LUCY & TOM
GO TO SCHOOL

written and drawn by Shirley Hughes

VICTOR GOLLANCZ LIMITED · LONDON · 1980

Lucy and Tom were two little children who were not yet old enough to go to school. When it was fine they played in the garden. They liked to look over the gate and see what was happening in the street.

Often Lucy would get out
her dolls and have a pretend
school. Lucy was the teacher
and if Tom was in a good
mood he would be one of
the class.

But sometimes,
especially when it rained,
Lucy was bored.
She was tired of
playing with Tom.
She was tired of her toys.

Her mother said that as she was nearly five she would soon be going
to a real school.

Lucy had her school things ready. She had a new grey skirt, a pair of brown shoes, a pencil case and a satchel. Tom wished that he had a satchel too.

Lucy and Tom knew where the school was. They had seen the boys and girls going in, and heard them shouting at playtime.

On the first day of school Lucy held her mother's hand very tightly. In the school playground there were a great many children waiting to go in. They saw Lucy's friend Jane. She was peeping out from behind her mother and holding on to her coat.

In the cloakroom Mum helped Lucy find her peg and hang up her jacket. Lucy's peg had her name and a picture of a teddy above it.

In the classroom was
a smiling teacher. She
was writing down
names.
She said, "Hello Lucy!
Hello Jane!"
She was called
Miss Walker.

The classroom was full of children and a great many interesting things to look at. There was a little shop with pretend money.

Lucy and Jane started to play in the
shop with three other little girls.

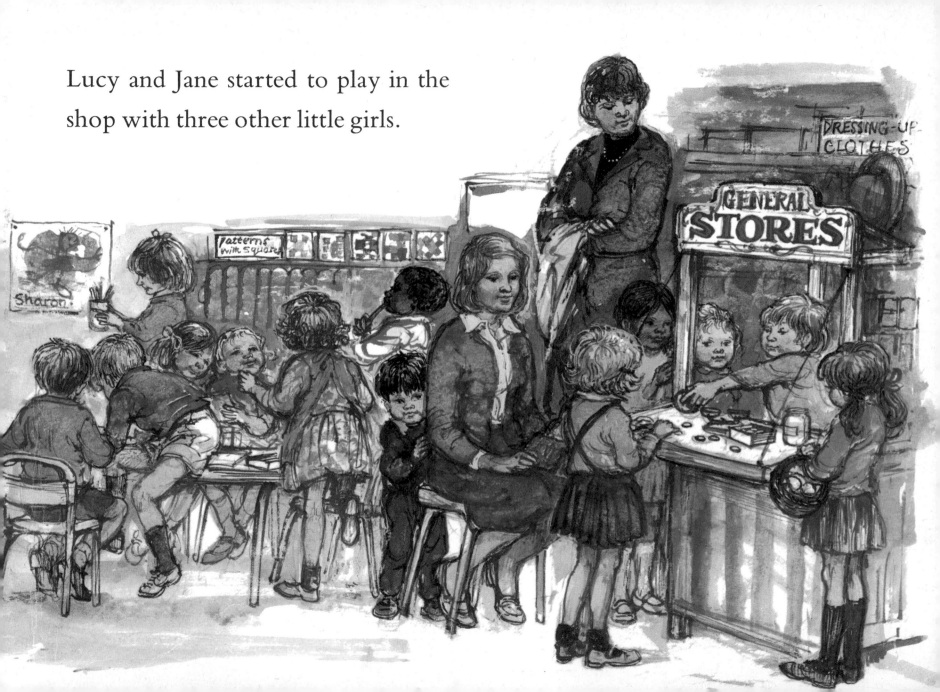

The mothers watched for a while. When it was time for them to go and get on with *their* shopping Jane did not want them to leave.

Lucy's mother gave her a hug and said, "See you at dinner time. Look after Jane won't you?"

Lucy wasn't feeling specially brave, but she took Jane's hand.

Tom yelled on the way out because *he* wanted to go to school too.

At playtime Lucy had some milk with a straw.

The playground was very noisy. Some children were playing games.

Some were fighting, some were chasing about and some were walking

with their arms round each other.

Jane had an apple. She gave Lucy a bite and they had a quiet game

in a corner.

After playtime Miss Walker read a story. They thought she was a very nice teacher indeed.

Later Lucy sorted some shells and coloured a picture.

"What did you do this morning, now I am a schoolgirl?" Lucy asked Tom at dinner time. Tom had done some colouring too.

Lucy's best thing at school was music and movement. She liked pretending to be a tiny mouse and then growing into a huge giant.

She liked it when they dressed up and acted their stories.

She liked Assembly too, because of the hymns.

Lucy's worst thing at school was a boy called Neil Bailey who kept pushing her in the playground.
Some days Lucy looked forward to going to school and some days she did not want to go very much, but she soon got used to it.

Now Tom was bored at home. He missed Lucy and she was often too tired to play when she came home from school. He followed Mum about wanting something to do.

Mum said that Tom could
join a playgroup in the
mornings. She bought him
a satchel just like Lucy's.
He put into it some pencils
and cars and his old
Teddy.

At the playgroup Tom painted and sang and played with toys and clay. There were plenty of boys and girls there to be his friends.

Tom liked the playgroup so much that he ran ahead of Mum every morning to get there first. Now Tom was a schoolboy too!

© Shirley Hughes 1973
First published October 1973
Second impression August 1977
Third impression October 1980
ISBN 0 575 01689 2
Printed in Great Britain by Ebenezer Baylis & Son Ltd, Leicester and London